A ... Holidays
MEMORIAL DAY

Connor Dayton

PowerKiDS
press.

New York

Published in 2012 by The Rosen Publishing Group, Inc.
29 East 21st Street, New York, NY 10010

First Edition

Editor: Jennifer Way
Book Design: Julio Gil

Photo Credits: Cover, p. 23 Ariel Skelley/age fotostock; pp. 4–5 © www.iStockphoto.com/Eileen Hart; pp. 7, 9, 19, 24 (top right) Shutterstock.com; pp. 11, 24 (top left) Mark Wilson/Getty Images; pp. 13, 24 (bottom right) Joshua Roberts-Pool/Getty Images; p. 15 Kris Connor/Getty Images; pp. 17, 24 (bottom left) Tim Yuan/Shutterstock.com; pp. 20–21 Robert Laberge/Getty Images.

Library of Congress Cataloging-in-Publication Data

Dayton, Connor.
Memorial Day / by Connor Dayton. — 1st ed.
    p. cm. — (American holidays)
Includes index.
ISBN 978-1-4488-6143-9 (library binding) — ISBN 978-1-4488-6244-3 (pbk.) — ISBN 978-1-4488-6245-0 (6-pack)
1. Memorial Day—Juvenile literature. I. Title.
E642.D39 2012
394.262—dc23
                              2011022341

Manufactured in the United States of America

CPSIA Compliance Information: Batch #WW12PK: For Further Information contact Rosen Publishing, New York, New York at 1-800-237-9932

Contents

What Is Memorial Day?   4

A Meaningful Holiday   6

Memorial Day Fun   14

Words to Know   24

Index   24

Web Sites   24

Memorial Day is the last
Monday in May.

This holiday honors soldiers who died serving America.

Flags fly at **half-staff** on Memorial Day morning. This is done for fallen soldiers.

People visit graves on Memorial Day.

The president places a **wreath** at Arlington National **Cemetery**, in Virginia.

The National Memorial Day
Concert is in Washington, D.C.

Cities have Memorial Day **parades**.

Families have Memorial
Day picnics.

The Indianapolis 500 is held on Memorial Day. This is a big car race.

Memorial Day is the start of summer fun!

Words to Know

cemetery

half-staff

parade

wreath

Index

P
people, 10
president, 12

R
race, 20

S
soldiers, 6, 8

W
Washington
D.C., 14

Web Sites

Due to the changing nature of Internet links, PowerKids Press has developed an online list of Web sites related to the subject of this book. This site is updated regularly. Please use this link to access the list:

www.powerkidslinks.com/amh/memorial